I0771257

ANDY TYRA

# CAVERNS

## *below*

# MILWAUKEE

# Caverns Below Milwaukee

Written and illustrated by Andy Tyra



Visit AndyTyra.com

**ISBN** 979-8-9859956-0-2

For all the believers
in Milwaukee.

# 1

## SACRED ARTIFACTS

His birth name was Walter but everyone knew Grandpa as Papa Chuck. His huge personality left an equally large void in our family when he died. I was seven when he had his stroke but the few memories I have of him are vivid. He made pizzas while singing along to oldies on the radio. He peeled and ate an orange during his nightly game shows. He joked with his brothers and fishing buddies on a phone that was also a table lamp. The white ceramic contraption sat on a side table next to Papa Chuck's recliner. Installed in the base was a rotary phone with a coiled cord and a handset as big as a dumbbell. My older brother Kevin and I used to make prank calls on it, asking people if they knew where we could buy "potato boots" which were not a thing.

Shortly after his funeral, my brother and I each received a box that contained some of Papa Chuck's effects. My box held three black-and-white photos in an envelope: a shiny-haired high school portrait, a snapshot of young Walter looking tough in dirty coveralls while leaning on a station wagon, and one with him and my Grandma Myrna on a picnic blanket. There were also a half dozen pristine cowboy-themed comic books in plastic and a pair of old brown shoes.

I was too young to appreciate the value. It may as well have been a box of wet sandwiches. But when I rediscovered my shoe box among the

Aral's
Shoe Repair

artifacts in my Mom's basement, it was like finding lost treasure.

The brown shoes popped into my mind when I was trying to figure out what to wear to Kevin's wedding in June. I was so broke in my early twenties that buying a decent pair of new shoes was not in the budget. The wedding was a couple of months away and there was no way I could wear sneakers or my work uglies — the comfortable black blocks that were part of my restaurant uniform since high school. The wingtips would be a good match for my new suit and provide a way for Papa Chuck to attend the wedding, if only through the spirit of his surviving footwear.

The problem was that the shoes were stiff and crusty to the extent that wearing them would likely result in their total destruction. I decided to visit the shoe repair place on Howell Avenue to see if they could work some magic.

Back then I was a server at a breakfast-and-lunch spot in Bay View called The Tiptop and I also cleaned up after hours at a restaurant in St. Francis called Fancy Dan's. So I had trouble getting to the cobbler's shop during their operating hours which were Tuesday through Thursday from 11 a.m. to 4 p.m. as dictated on their cassette-driven answering machine. It was a narrow window by my service industry standards, so it took me a while to get there.

It was a mystery how businesses like Aral's Shoe Repair could exist at all. They had no website or social media presence. While the world around them had picked up speed, they were just cobbling along, continuing to practice a lost art despite the challenges to their business model.

Online, most reviewers gave them 2 or 3 stars and suggested that the cobblers weren't great at customer service. One critical consumer, FarisonHorde, commented, "The guy is rude. Said my $200 shoes are cheap plastic." Two outliers gave 4 stars and provided more positive feedback. KingJakeDaffy wrote "Great service by strange people" while PB&J227 stated "My cowboy boots are better than new. Definitely recommend these guys."

I've always assumed that a city with sufficient population could support some number of old-timey artisans — cobblers, clockmakers, upholsters and the like — if they had a decent amount of traffic going

OYEES
NLY

past their shops. The peeling sign hanging in front of Aral's Shoe Repair made me think this hypothesis wasn't true in this case. It didn't appear to be a functioning business at all. The sign was small and hard to see in the context of its brick background. Like many former bars in Milwaukee, the building had a corner entrance. Theirs was void of any additional signage and flanked by large windows with blinds closed.

Inside I found an ongoing conversation between the shopkeeper and a woman wearing a cheetah print jacket over a black suit. The cobbler, a very pale man of around fifty-years-old with long, sterling hair, told her in a calm voice that reattaching a strap on her heels would be a waste of time because they were made from "just plastic and glue."

The woman bottled her outrage and collected her shoes. She left behind a perfumed scent that was soon replaced by ambient chemical odors comprised of two parts laundromat and one part auto body shop.

"Just one moment," the man said and entered an adjacent room where tinny music and television applause blared.

The counter was old-school Formica worn from years of gentle abrasion. There was a coat tree with a few jackets and a baseball hat on top. I owned the same hat.

After a moment, a sinewy woman with a stern face emerged from the back room and shouted behind her. Her skin and hair were as pale as her male counterpart.

"If you can't take it, ask Wick. It needs to be in Chortle tomorrow."

While I was trying to process what the female shopkeeper was talking about, she lifted a hefty brown ledger from underneath the counter and slapped it down. In a series of tidy movements, she opened the book and wrote something, then clapped it shut.

"Yes?" she asked.

"Hi. I was hoping you could do something with these."

The shopkeeper examined the wingtips thoroughly, lifting the tongue of each shoe and looking inside. She scratched the leather with a fingernail.

"We can fix these," she concluded. The origin of her accent was unclear. Maybe Pennsylvania Dutch.

"Pick up on Tuesday."

She wrote on a slip of paper and handed it to me.

Shoes.
Pick up on 5/17
You have
bad breath.
BELIEVE

# 2

## MAGICAL THINKING

My alarm went off on the following Tuesday and I snoozed it for two hours before getting a coffee and going to the cobbler shop. The female shopkeeper closed the big brown book as I opened the door.

"Hi, I'm—"

"Nine dollars."

I pulled cash from my wallet and she fetched Papa Chuck's wingtips, which gave me a moment to revisit their business model. A few days per week, a handful of customers came in and paid between nine and twenty dollars. Even if they got a spike in profits for repairing equestrian gear or leather furniture, it still didn't add up. Maybe they were committed to keeping the family business alive or they owned the building and didn't need much money to live. Or maybe they produced fake versions of designer handbags in the back room.

I checked out the various footwear on the front shelf: a pair of purple clogs, some chukkas with metal studs around the collar, sharp-toed slingbacks and weathered baby shoes with buckles. No baby would wear shoes like that. I took out my phone and tapped two quick photos, then stuck it back in my pocket.

She clopped Papa's wingtips on the counter. They had been restored to gleaming perfection.

"Wow. They look so good!"

The creases were smoothed as was the moonscape of the toe cap. Every surface was made new while retaining the original character. The spot on the toe where the cherry of a cigarette sizzled a black divot was now just a bump.

I dug out three dollars to offer as a tip.

"We don't accept tips," she said, taking the money anyway, and passed me my receipt.

I couldn't get over the miraculous restoration. The wingtips were placed in the most visible location in my apartment: on a dish towel in the middle of my kitchen table. The disbelief and resulting joy were renewed each time I passed.

At the wedding, the shoes outpaced all expectations. My girlfriend Jess and my Aunt Lauryl both commented on them. Jess said that I could have been a suit model "for an outlet store," which was more than adequate praise for my needs. It gave me enough confidence to get beyond my anxiety and enjoy myself. I hugged my new sister-in-law and apologized for being so sour at a baseball game months before. In my speech at the reception, I told my brother what a good choice he made. Jess and I danced to a slow song and kissed in a dim hallway afterward. When I ordered my last brandy old fashioned, I said to myself "thanks, Papa Chuck" and drank it in four swallows.

Jess had already left for work when I woke up with my trousers still on. I cleaned the shoes with a sock and returned them to the kitchen table, still impressed by the degree to which they had been repaired. In my hangover fuzz, it felt like a mystery to be solved.

Who were these cobblers? I studied the photos on my phone. The weathered baby shoes were too tiny for a toddler yet their aggressive treads were worn down from thousands of steps. I'd always wondered why they made hiking boots for babies at all but seeing such footwear in need of repair took the absurdity to the next level.

It was too peculiar for me to leave it be. It formed a loop in my mind that, in retrospect, I should have broken with some physical activity. When the female cobbler said something about "Chortle," she was implying that it was a location and not just a kind of snorty laughter. A search revealed nothing. It wasn't the name of any place on earth as far as I could tell. I surrendered to my hangover and slept through the afternoon.

The following night, Jess and I went out for chicken mole at Amuletos and I showed her the photos. She looked distracted as I held my phone across the table. It could have been a lot of different things on her mind. She didn't vocalize everything on her mind the way I did but I was surprised she didn't have anything to say about the wingtips or the tiny buckle shoes.

"These are the baby shoes I told you about. Zoom in."

She was staring at the small painting mounted above the bar mirror: a portrait of a forlorn toddler with a pageboy hairdo.

"Unbelievable."

It was clear that she wasn't talking about the portrait but I was unsure about whether her comment conveyed veiled amusement or hidden judgment regarding my topic of choice. I assumed it was the former.

"I know! The baby who wore those shoes must have hiked the Appalachian Trail."

"I bet they are leprechaun shoes."

It was hidden judgment. Whenever Jess mentioned leprechauns, they were a placeholder for those things that she considered foolish. I deflected her comment with laughter, knowing the joke was on her. Leprechauns were known to be cobblers themselves and could fix their own shoes.

We returned to her house and watched a show about unlikely animal friends. We laughed a few times before she fell asleep on the sofa. I covered her with an afghan and researched the origin of the word "Aral." It had Turkish and Indian origins. It was a surname and a somewhat common first name. Different sources defined the word as a stream between two mountains, a descriptor for curled objects, the resin of a shala tree or an elephant in rut.

Jess would say I was taking it too far. She would remind me of my ghost hunting expedition in West Allis or the Sasquatch trap at the Kettle Moraine that almost got me arrested.

The world was full of bizarre undercurrents that moved unseen and Milwaukee was full of them. Those kinds of mysteries and supernatural phenomena looked so much more exotic against the bohemian backdrop of my hometown. Every bar, hotel and bowling alley had multiple ghost stories. Frozen alligators were found in alleys. Unexpected sinkholes swallowed automobiles whole. Raccoons traveled in the sewer like goblins in an underworld labyrinth.

My pal Delvin and I were seniors in high school when we stopped for ice cream at a place on the East Side. It had been raining for days and we were bored of it, thus the senseless need for candy bar bits suspended in soft serve. We stopped at a stoplight when we felt a quake that shook the car. There was a metallic clunk like knuckles colliding at a rail yard and a black SUV a few cars ahead dropped through a sinkhole. It crunched into the deep dark rubble twelve or fifteen feet below, severing a sewer pipe on its way down. Delvin panicked and almost hit the car in front of us with his sudden U-turn. It seemed plausible that the sinkhole might spread and we'd all fall through the street.

Incredibly, local news would later report that the sinkhole driver was okay. But motorists would forever know that potential danger lurked beneath the street.

Later that night, Delvin stopped on Russell Avenue and pointed at the roof of a house where three raccoons were perched on the ridge, silhouetted like gargoyles with wiggly little hands.

"They usually move around in the storm drains but they don't know where to go when the system gets full like this. They climb trees and telephone poles and stuff. One time I saw them hiding out in the playground at the Trowbridge school."

Delvin's claim was verified the following summer when I saw a raccoon waddling down the margin of Clement Avenue just after dusk. It poked its head into the curb drain and oozed through the slot like a glop of magma.

It made me think about how strange things are happening everywhere, all the time. While we slept, unknown deep sea creatures were feeding and being fed upon. Dragonfly nymphs were breathing through gills in their anuses. So was it so far-fetched to think something extraordinary was behind the rebirth of Papa Chuck's wingtips? I resolved to find more shoes in need of repair.

# 3

## TREAD CAREFULLY

Jess and I woke to thunder and tiny raindrops tapping the windows. We got up, made coffee and visited a thrift store before it started pouring. We found a weathered pair of Chelsea boots with cracks above the toe box and brought them back to my apartment to take some "before" photos.

In the end, it was hard to tell if Jess was amused or annoyed by my fixation. Her natural resting state was so wry that it was possible she was inwardly entertained by it. When I told her that I discovered the names of the shop owners on a Wisconsin database of registered businesses — Aral and Virda Green — she said nothing and checked her phone.

We ate Thai takeout and started a movie she had mentioned a couple of weeks before. Halfway through, she tossed me the remote, put her shoes on and went home early.

I took the boots to Aral's the following day and tried to observe every trifle.

The cobbler stood at the counter clad in an apron and a baseball hat that held back his long white hair. He had the look of a freewheeling retiree who might also be into jam bands. He was braiding three strips of orange leather but stopped to greet me.

"Good morning."

Pick up
your Boots
on
Wednesday

"Hi. Are you Aral?"

He confirmed with a nod and rotated the boots on the counter to evaluate them.

"I'm David," I said, trying to sound nonchalant.

"Glad to know you, David."

He seemed friendly enough, in contrast to my previous visit when he had told a customer that her shoes were made of rubbish.

"I can mend these," Aral said

The rhythmic steps of someone descending a staircase preceded Virda's appearance. She motioned to Aral and he handed her the braided band. She evaluated his work then shrugged before picking up one of the Chelsea boots and sniffing it.

"Huh. Thrift store."

Aral passed me a slip of paper and Virda took the boots to the next room.

There it was again: the sound of television applause and impish laughter on the other side of the door. This time I glimpsed a child with a dark brown ponytail and a poncho. She was wearing the black buckle shoes, now shiny and perfect. The door shut before I could take a photo so I waited with my camera aimed at the door. It opened just partially and Virda was staring at me through the crack. Her death stare on my screen gave me a pulse of adrenaline.

"Run away child, and do not return!" Virda shouted as I fled.

That afternoon at work my tips were pathetic and I screwed up a few orders. Virda's words got in my head. I was sorry for being so nosy but couldn't shake the feeling that they were hiding something.

My place was silent when I got home. I ate cereal in the solemn company of Papa Chuck's wingtips but stopped crunching when I saw something white and pointy protruding from one of the shoes: a small paper airplane. Someone had also opened the kitchen window a couple of inches to deliver it. The message inside seemed to be either a warning or a threat.

I almost told Jess about it but decided to wait. Instead I texted her and we made plans to have dinner on Tuesday.

Afterward I locked all the doors and windows. I paced around the kitchen thinking about the note.

Tread
Carefully.

# 4

## CONVINCE YOURSELF OF ANYTHING

My friend Evan said more than once that "people can convince themselves of absolutely anything." One didn't have to look very far to see people fooling themselves, making certainty out of scraps. Even though I agreed, it was still hard for me to reconcile. Extraordinary things *were* possible, however unlikely, and there were gaps in human knowledge that left big mysteries unsolved despite our probing. The space between these ideas left just enough room in the realm of possibility for creatures like the Hodag, the horned beast sighted in Rhinelander, and Richfield's equally legendary Goatman.

Jess was a true skeptic, so my tendency to believe in things without unequivocal evidence drove her crazy. She knew about all of my most cringeworthy examples of self-delusion except the worst one. It happened at the Lion Horse, a historic bar in Riverwest that hosted a rotating series of classic pinball machines. Evan and I went there every week or so to play *Attack from Mars* and have a few drinks.

A local character called Cherry, whose real name was Jerry, was also a regular there. He had a thick goatee and wore a red Donegal hat with matching suspenders. He was known for whiskey-fueled blather that mixed conspiracy theories, anecdotes and pseudoscience into a muddy stew. His rants were peppered with euphemisms like "play nug-a-nug"

and "beat a bear at checkers" which would have made him charming if he hadn't been so obnoxious. Truth is, we might have forgiven all of that but he was also known to pocket tips left on the bar when he thought no one was looking.

The first time I experienced full-throttle Cherry was when he was sitting at the bar, going off about hidden cameras in TV screens. He got so fired up that he spit a piece of popcorn into another guy's mouth. The victim turned green and exited while Cherry continued his diatribe, oblivious about what had happened.

Hearing his voice or seeing his hat at the bar was a reason to go somewhere else — and we did try to avoid him — but we couldn't avoid his impressive scores. The best pinball tables at Lion Horse, Chargas Inn and Wild Bramble had at least two instances of the initials J-E-R at the top of their high score lists.

When I asked about Cherry, Evan told me, "That guy sucks. He's not nice to the pins."

Evan was always polite and reserved so his opinion carried some weight. Sure enough, I later witnessed Cherry shoving tables hard enough to tax the fasteners that held the legs on without triggering a tilt. I wanted to give him the benefit of the doubt but he wore me down too.

I remember one night when a local sax virtuoso was playing in harmony with old soul songs on the jukebox. It was a singular and beautiful Milwaukee moment that we couldn't enjoy because Cherry wouldn't shut up. He was spouting off about "flatware," claiming that the arcade company had installed a magnetic device on the underside of *Pirate's Booty* just to shorten his game. Other tables like *Theater of Magic* employed such hardware but it was an aspect of the overall theme rather than a hustle.

"These guys are getting good at stealing my money!" he hollered over a sax-infused exaltation of an '80s classic.

Cherry slipped off a tall chair in mid-sentence, sending him to the floor. People laughed and watched him flounder while the music continued. Evan helped him up.

When *Pirate's Booty* went missing later that year, those of us in the Milwaukee pinball community pointed at the most likely suspect. Stealing a pinball machine was the sort of crime that fit his character.

Cherry was vocal about his innocence and even though no evidence was found to implicate him, everyone was sure that he did it. When the arcade company threatened to take their machines out of the Lion Horse, Cherry became a scapegoat.

Only later did I realize our assumption of guilt failed to consider some key details. One: he had bad knees and struggled to climb stairs. Two: according to Jack, the Lion Horse's bartender, Cherry had no close friends or family. In fact, Jack's sympathy was the primary reason Cherry's antics were tolerated to the degree they were. Three: he had no money. The stolen bills were hardly enough to pay his bar bill.

This wasn't a man with resources. He would've required help lifting and loading the three-hundred-pound pinball machine and some degree of agility — or a nimble accomplice — to climb up on the bar and cover the security camera. Even if he had a friend or a sibling he could rely on, it was hard to imagine Cherry persuading anyone to assist with such a heist without a considerable incentive.

The bartender said there was no damage anywhere in the bar and as far as anyone could tell, not one bottle was missing. There was also a tip jar left out and it had been untouched.

Insurance money quieted the arcade company. *Pirate's Booty* was never recovered and Cherry disappeared from the Lion Horse, leaving only his high scores as evidence of his existence.

Not long after, I passed him while riding my bike near the Milwaukee Art Museum. His mouth hung open like a ghoul as he pulled a small cart loaded with duffel bags and a fishing pole. His face brightened with recognition when he saw me. He must have known my face if not my name but I was too stunned to speak. I still regret not saying hello.

Did he not deserve the benefit of the doubt? It would have cost nothing and required very little effort on my part to defend him from the bullies that cast him out of the tribe. It's hard to understand the thin partitions that separate a person from one path or another but I believe I could have helped Cherry if I hadn't assumed the worst in him.

# 5

## CHASING LEPRECHAUNS

Tuesday night was lovely. Jess made moussaka according to a family recipe and it was cinnamony, savory perfection. I brought baklava from Poulos Bakery, one of her top three treats, and we agreed that it was a quintessential spring evening.

We laughed about a headline from *The Onion*, then I told her that I had gotten caught taking pictures at the cobbler's shop and showed her the paper airplane. By the time we had dessert, her smile had left altogether.

"Can we talk about something besides shoe repair?"

"Okay," I tried not to sound unhinged. "You don't think it's weird that they broke in to deliver a little note?"

"How do you know it was them? Maybe one of your friends did it. Or some other enemy."

"It's in Virda's handwriting."

She sighed and poured herself more wine.

"It's super weird!"

"I just think there are other things that you should be focusing on."

Our good mood floated up and away like an underwater bubble. I had always thought that Jess and I were perfect complements. I was the comedian to her straight man and she was the backbeat to my

CUSTOMER
PARKING
OTHERS TOWED

yakety sax. Now it seemed like I was a pathetic manchild and she was the mature adult. Jess had an open heart, a positive attitude and grace when it came to navigating social situations. She worked at her mother's PR firm, took business classes and played softball on Wednesdays. It sounded exhausting to me. My life was a space walk that I viewed from inside an insulated bubble while remaining unavailable to all but a select few. This left plenty of time for pinball, trivia nights and Sasquatch documentaries.

I asked if she wanted to take a walk around Humboldt Park. Nope. She was meeting her friend Erin at the beer garden and would call me later. I loaded a whole piece of baklava into my mouth and walked home.

My trust issues had caused problems in the past, so I steered clear of the beer garden. I wanted to call my brother but he was on his honeymoon in Cozumel. I opted for a long bike ride to nowhere in particular.

The rumbling and impacts coming from Thunder Haus told me someone was bowling in the basement but I didn't stop for a drink. Instead I cut through the park before zigzagging back home on side streets. The ride helped me galvanize my feelings about Jess. I wasn't going to suppress my curiosity because it annoyed someone nor did I want to annoy her. If she no longer had patience for the oddball things that inspired me, I couldn't imagine we would ever be on the same page. It wasn't a big surprise but it hurt.

Due to my habit of not drinking enough water, my tongue was as dry as a pine cone but I told myself I would chug tap water after one quick stop. Leaning my bike on the bus stop shelter, I pretended to look at my phone and I zoomed my camera to see through Aral's front window, past the open blinds where he was cobbling at his workbench. He drilled a hole in a wooden panel, sanded the burrs, then blew away the dust. He repeated that several times before sipping from a rocks glass and glancing out the window.

Spooked, I moved to flee but my kickstand got wedged in the pedal assembly. My bike toppled and I fell on my backpack, crushing a chocolate chip cookie that I was saving for later. A teen with headphones laughed at me. Jess was right. I was a fool chasing leprechauns.

Aral was at the door, shouting my name and signaling for me to come over. He called so many times that it was impossible to pretend I didn't notice him.

Soon I was sitting at his workbench, explaining how I forgot to drink water that day while he poured me a cup of hot jasmine tea. In terms of beverages to drink after a bike ride, it wasn't my top choice but I was really thirsty and forced it down.

"You should not forget the water. No water makes you clumsy."

I nodded in tight-lipped agreement.

"Automobiles can kill you when you are clumsy. Predators can also."

His logic was sound, even if it was rather morbid. He refilled my mug from a kettle and refilled his rocks glass from a decanter of amber liquid that might have been whiskey or brandy.

"Is Virda here?"

"She is away," he said, amused. "She did tell me about the camera."

He made the thumb and first finger of each hand into corners of a rectangle to pantomime either a smartphone or the shape of a photo.

Their lack of knowledge about something as basic as photography lent credence to my theory that they had Amish or Mennonite roots.

"Sorry about the photos. I wanted to show my girlfriend your beautiful work. Everyone takes photos of everything nowadays — but I understand that you don't like it."

A smile crawled over his face.

"No cameras please. But if you respect shoecraft, perhaps you wish to be a cobbler?"

"I don't know. What were you cobbling?"

"*Hobsandals.*"

Aral handed me a peanut-shaped footbed with a dozen holes in it. It was as curved, as long as my forearm and had carved-in arch support. He threaded a cord through the holes to create a primitive-looking sandal.

"Take off your shoes."

He placed the plank under my green sock and secured the cord around my ankle with a few wraps and a knot. It looked ridiculous but it was quite comfortable. I hopped and walked around the shop as a quick test drive.

"Good, yes?"

"Yeah. I usually don't wear sandals with socks but they're comfortable."

I removed the sandals and Aral walked over to the frontmost green shelf.

While unattended, I resisted his urge to take a photo of his workspace.

He returned carrying the restored Chelsea boots. They were glossy and unblemished. I looked at them, then back to Aral, then back to the boots.

"Wow!"

They looked magnificent.

Aral took my twenty dollars and followed me to the door.

I fumbled with the stubborn zipper of my backpack trying to stash the shoes for the ride home while Aral selected a key on his key ring and prepared to lock the door behind me.

"Goodnight, David. Please stay hydrated."

I wanted to ask him about the paper airplane but all of a sudden I felt nervous.

My partially closed backpack slipped from my hand and plopped on the floor. I snatched it up and forced the zipper closed as I mustered by courage.

"I wanted to ask you something. Did you send this?"

I handed him the paper airplane. He unfolded it, studied it for a few seconds and wrinkled his forehead with concern before passing it back.

"You should go."

# 6

## A HOLE IN ROCK BOTTOM

Automobiles were indeed a danger to clumsy people. Less than a block away from my house, I managed to snag my handlebar on the side view mirror of a parked car. The resulting crash — my second bicycle accident in two hours — tweaked my neck and gave me a cut above my right eye that bled like crazy.

I walked home, took a shower and watched many episodes of *The Simpsons*. I knew I shouldn't fall asleep in case I had a concussion, so every so often I tapped a button on a little plastic fob that made four different Sasquatch noises. It turned into a game wherein I muted the television and pressed a button on the fob to replace a bit of dialogue with a throaty bellow or a feral snort-and-sniff.

My mom phoned me and I told her everything was great. I checked the mailbox while she told me about her taekwondo class and how the teacher was so handsome. She asked if I would help her carry two boxes down to the basement storage area and I said I would. My mailbox contained two pieces of junk mail and a letter from Jess. She had never sent me a letter, so in the back of my mind I knew it could be bad. Another part of me didn't buy into my own dread. I entertained the notion that it contained tickets to a show at The Pabst Theater.

"Gotta go, Mom. Love you."

David,

I'm so sorry but we can't be together anymore.

Not as anything more then friends.

It is clear that we are becoming two very different people. I hope that you find what you are looking for.

Jess

A card fell on the kitchen table when I unfolded the letter. It was a business card for a therapist in the Third Ward. I crumpled it into a ball tighter than a collapsing star, and pitched it to the floor.

Jess wrote in the letter that we were two different people. Obviously. All of us pull up our own underwear. What she meant was that we weren't similar enough for her to tolerate me nor I to endure her criticism. She had a 401K whereas I believed that DNA evidence would one day surface and prove the existence of the Goatman. She was the sort of person who didn't know the difference between "then" and "than" even as she wrote her own success story. I'd always value good grammar and look for ghostly children in dark hallways.

It wasn't sealed or addressed so I knew she had hand-delivered it to my mailbox. She must have considered a face-to-face breakup and decided it wasn't worth the drama. This time we were on the same page.

I returned to my porch chair and monitored the streaky clouds that slid across the twilight star field. My bicycle remained on the sidewalk with its bent front rim and misaligned handlebars. I didn't blink for a long time.

The next morning I fumbled my phone into the sink while washing dishes. I was trying to text a fellow server to see if she could cover my shift. It seemed appropriate considering the hideous cut on my face covered with gauze and a piece of packing tape.

I went to work anyway. My coworkers asked what happened and I provided bogus explanations that included "I slipped on a burrito," "bad day at clown college" and simply "diarrhea." Charlotte, the restaurant's owner, was disgusted either by my humor or my face and suggested I go home.

"Customers don't need to see that."

Her words had no effect. It didn't matter who was concerned or exasperated. My elevator had deposited me at rock bottom, a place where my apathy flattened everything and everyone into a featureless plane. What I would realize later was that there was a hole through the bedrock of rock bottom that led to damp passageways and caverns that smelled like a pickle factory.

My shift was almost over when I noticed Virda's distinctive silhouette up front in the window seat.

"Hey clown college, I got a salad here for the lady at table two," John the cook snapped.

"That's not my section."

"Take it to two."

I forced a smile and approached her.

"Virda! Hey, it's David...from the store. I was walking through the kitchen and I think I found lunch."

My words were those of an oily salesman but it was the best I could do. That voice combined with my face must have been quite a sight.

"Zounds, David," she said with a sardonic smile, "That looks like it hurts."

"Oh, it's not so bad," I lied.

She seemed pleased by my state of injury.

"Do me a favor, will you? Dispose of this?"

She offered me a familiar sandwich bag that contained a crumbled chocolate chip cookie but dropped it on the floor before I could grab it.

"Th-that thing. It must have slipped out of my backpack."

"Do not visit my shop again."

"Absolutely. I didn't mean to...I mean...Aral invited me in."

She forked her salad as I stammered.

"Shtay away," she said, chewing.

I stuffed the cookie bag into my black waist apron and retreated. When I looked back, she was glaring at me, still chewing.

• • • • •

Blame was a funny thing. It seemed natural to avoid it or spread it to others who could share the load. Meanwhile, the actual events remain unchanged.

I would have liked to blame somebody else for the way things played out but my own choices were the real reason I fell into failure. I did some things. I said some things. I had convinced myself of things and made some choices and here I was.

It was me who was creeping around Aral's Shoe Repair, taking pictures and acting a fool. My behavior was every bit as suspicious as a paper airplane in a shoe. Even if the cobbler shop was a front for trafficking bushmeat, they had a right to their privacy.

My boss Charlotte wasn't to blame either. She found me in the hallway near the time clock, pressed flat against the wall like an escaped convict. Beyond acting like a lunatic, my attitude had been horrible for a long time and I was always late. I would have fired me. The other shoe dropped on my second job a few days later when I forgot to show up for one shift and then another.

Everyone else had become flat extras in my story, walking around my featureless plane. Beyond that, Virda could have pressed charges for trespassing, as my therapist in the Third Ward would later point out.

I also couldn't blame my landlord for kicking me out. My rent was one month behind for over a year until it reached two months. Frank had a big heart. Evan called him Diamond Box Frank because he once gave us great seats to a baseball game. But even a guy with a big heart needed money to survive. My carelessness pushed him beyond what was reasonable and that was my fault. My bad decisions stared back at me like the portrait of the forlorn toddler at Amuletos.

One night while playing *Medieval Madness* at Wild Bramble, I asked Evan if I was a fool. The question itself sounded emotionally needy and pathetic to my own ears. I knew it wasn't a fair question but his were sound opinions and I trusted his good sense. I needed a good sense answer and some empirical truth from which I could propel myself forward. Deep in every cell of my valves and ventricles, I knew that most things were beautiful or ugly only because people say they are — but beyond that I assumed there was some standard of foolishness that was non-negotiable. If so, where did I stand in relation to it?

"Nah. Just a bad ball. You'll get another chance."

"I don't mean the game. I'm talking generally. Am I doomed to be a fool forever?"

"You have a good heart. You just don't know it yet."

Translation: "You can convince yourself of absolutely anything."

Tres Mas
ORIGIN
Tres Mas
ORIGIN
Tres Mas
RANC
Tres Mas
RANC
Tres
Tres
Tres Mas
PICANTE
Everyone's Favorite
Ev
Fav

# 7

## BOTTLES IN THE BASEMENT

It was the first week of August when I moved back to my mom's house. I had finally become the manchild living with his mother that I always knew I could be.

I scored a job at the Hispanic grocery store in my mom's neighborhood where I used to buy chili-infused candy as a kid. It provided daily access to a top notch taqueria and an ever-changing gallery of colorful piñatas that I considered paper sculptures.

My top joy was perusing the store's shelves of seven-day prayer candles that were available for every conceivable purpose. One part of the inventory was of the religious variety, papered with images of saints or the Virgin Mary. The second category of candles had images of celebrities in place of the religious figures. The remainder were spell candles. They had illustrations rendered in a style that appealed to me. It was similar to tattoo art or old tarot cards. One could burn a red candle labeled with linked gold rings to bring back one's true love or burn a black candle labeled with a sword and some kind of ceremonial ribbon to keep someone away. I pondered whether the *Break Up* and the *Bring My Lover Back* candles burned simultaneously would cancel each other out.

When I brought a few prayer candles to the checkout, the cashier

CORTA MA
CEASE ALL EV
VELADORA COMPUE
bre Camino
ROAD OPENER
DORA COMPUESTA
PROTECTI
FROM ENEM
VELADORA COMPU

Miguel shook his head with disapproval. He wrapped each glass cylinder in paper and told me that they weren't a joke.

"Don't worry," I said, "I'll only use them for their sacred application...or to light sparklers."

Despite my awkwardness and failed attempts at humor, Miguel and I somehow became pals. He had a rare combination of quirks that jibed well with my own. He was self-deprecating and appreciated the same campy horror movies, psychedelic soul music and '80s hip-hop that I did. He came over for family dinners and to watch football on Sundays and afterwards we watched a selection from his huge collection of obscure anime. My family loved the guy.

I was fortunate that Miguel was willing to be my friend considering that he was way smarter than me. Such differentials don't often work. He had technical knowledge coupled with innate kindness, which meant that he used his deep knowledge about hacking, network security and surveillance responsibly. He once spent an hour trying to extract a spider from a bin of limes rather than letting it get squashed.

He showed me the security cameras he installed at the store and the multi-screen control room in the manager's office. He taught me a hundred things including how cryptocurrency worked and little known exploits of the CIA. In exchange, I introduced him to the amaretti cookies from my favorite bakery and the comedic potential of a remotely activated fart machine. On a few occasions, we put the device behind cereal boxes and watched through the security cameras as customers were surprised by a full spectrum of honks and squeaks. We laughed until we couldn't breathe.

We were both way closer to our moms than our dads. Miguel's dad hardly spoke a word when I came over to his house. His mom, however, was quick to laugh and effusive like my own mother.

My mom divorced my dad (whom I call Jeff) two years before she retired from her job as a legal assistant. Her journey to freedom started when my dad quit his job at a trucking company and adopted the persona of a motorcycle renegade. He had already been absent for most of our lives, driving for weeks at a stretch and home for a couple of days here and there. So when he left for good it wasn't as big of a trauma as it can be for other families. Jeff drank quite a lot but he wasn't he was never unruly. He helped pay the bills and came through at Christmas. He just never seemed satisfied with life at home. He didn't ask to see our report cards, never came to our baseball games and didn't care what we were interested in. It was as if any request for his time was an assault on his personal liberty, forcing my mom to pick up all the parental slack.

When I was in seventh grade, Mom had to work late and asked Jeff to pick me up after baseball practice. I sat on a curb until the sun started to set and it was clear he wasn't coming. No one answered when I called home from a pay phone so I walked home in the dark. When I asked Jeff about it later, he apologized without looking away from the television. He "just forgot" because he and my uncle were working on a custom chopper. That event was the perfect portrait of his character: absent, obsessed with motorcycles and sorry that he couldn't be bothered.

I had known that my mom was staying busy since the divorce. I mean, she told me that she was happy but I didn't fully understand her transformation until I lost everything and moved back home. It wasn't that she was simply happier as a single woman. Divorcing Jeff meant she had been totally reborn. She did things she had never done before. She took loads of classes at the Bay View Community Center: taekwondo, yoga, hip-hop dance, quilting. She went on movie dates with her friends to see whatever was playing at the Oriental Theater. She sang and danced around the house. Her buoyancy made my return feel less like a defeat and more like an exercise in healing. We played cribbage, made pesto and cracked crème brûlée. We talked and laughed like old friends. In an unexpected twist, my quality of life went way up.

It seemed like a good time to reboot myself, so I applied for a job as an Information Desk Assistant at the Milwaukee Public Library. I was glad to get an interview even though it didn't go very well. Early in the interview I revealed my lack of library experience and that I hadn't actually visited the library in years. My extreme anxiety about that revelation must have made it clear to my interviewer that I lacked the requisite people skills. I was sure there would be no callback.

My mom had come home from a workout and found me sulking on the sofa, nursing a beer in my formal interview duds.

"How did it go?"

"Not great."

"That's okay, David. Don't quit trying."

She saw Papa Chuck's wingtips by the door.

"Holy cow! Are those my dad's shoes?"

"Yeah. I thought you saw these at Kevin's wedding."

She was dazzled by the restoration, after having seen her father wear them for so many years. I explained that I took them to Aral's Shoe Repair and ended up telling her the whole story about the photos and how I was asked by Virda to never return.

"You just never know what people have been through," she said, "They probably didn't like you snooping around like that. It probably made 'em nervous."

She thought it unlikely that there was anything strange or criminal about their business. She compared Aral and Virda to our old neighbors, the Kowalczyks, who illegally snagged huge salmon from the Milwaukee River during spawning season.

"They would go to Hubbard Park and stock their freezer for the winter. For years they did that."

The Kowalczyks and the cobblers were not the same. George and Anne K brought survival skills from the old country. Aral and Virda were like aliens pretending to be human.

"I don't know. Something just seemed different about the cobblers. It's hard to explain."

When I related the story of the tiny buckle shoes with worn treads, I suspected my mom thought I was unhinged like Jess did.

"I love how you get so curious about things. You were always the creative one in the family."

She patted me on the top of the head and said goodnight.

The next day I woke up with my right eye scratchy and swollen shut. A couple of days later, my doctor told me I had shingles. I went straight to my room to convalesce while my mom called my boss to tell him I wouldn't be back to work for a while.

The headaches, itching and blisters were a sort of pain I had never felt before. Every time I closed my right eye, it felt like bits of glass were rolling under my eyelid. My mom came to my rescue a thousand times during that nightmarish period. I can't imagine trying to get through it without her. She played oldies on the stereo and taught me to do some yoga poses. I think she saved my life.

I couldn't help her shovel snow that winter but she insisted it was no problem.

"Helps me build up my core," she joked.

On one of my worst days, she helped me get a T-shirt over my head. It hurt like getting a tattoo but she coached me through it with calm confidence. Afterwards she brought me a glass of ice water and I held it to my face which was burning like a pizza roll right out of the oven. Then she sat on the side of my bed and tried to get me to laugh.

"Have you seen that man who walks his cat on our street?" she asked.

We laughed.

"Yeah, I talked to him once."

"He's nice and everything but next time you see him, watch how he doesn't move his arms."

"Haha. I never noticed."

"It's actually super hard to keep them still. Just walk down the hallway and try it. Your arms want to move."

I got out of bed and tried it. It was a scientific truth that legs walking want arms swinging. Her ability to make me laugh got me moving again.

A few months later I was sitting on the porch having a cruller and coffee when I overheard my mom talking to Aunt Lauryl on the phone inside. She told her sister about Aral's Shoe Repair. She also related the story about me taking photos and being told to stay away from the shop.

"I worry about him sometimes. He's probably gonna live with me forever."

The next day I was restocking cereal when I got the call from Kevin. His voice quivered when he told me the news.

"My mom had an accident! I gotta go!" I said to Miguel and my manager Bon as I ran out of the store.

The doctor said she had received fifteen stings in total, a number that would not have been life-threatening if she had not been allergic to wasp venom. We figured out that she disturbed an underground nest when she was mowing the lawn and the toxins took effect before she could find her EpiPen. Mom made it over to the neighbor's house and Shonda, our neighbor's daughter, drove her to the emergency room.

Kevin surmised that she might have died from anaphylactic shock if she had waited for an ambulance.

When I arrived at the hospital, they had already stabilized her breathing and heart rate. She was recovering but still looking pretty rough with all the tubes and apparatus. I sat myself on a green vinyl settee next to Kevin and his wife Daniela and we waited. Over the course of several hours, our butts became embedded in the hard cushions.

It was around 6 a.m. when the nurse told us that Mom was out of danger. We were relieved yet none of us could sleep. Kevin turned on the TV and muted the volume. All I could think about was how I should have mowed the lawn instead of letting Mom do it. Daniela reassured me that it wasn't my fault.

Flowers and sympathy balloons were delivered. A young man in scrubs brought in an arrangement of three white lilies. Kevin accepted them and read the card aloud.

"'Hope you're feeling better. From Virda.' Who's Virda?"

I thought about the timing of our recent calamities. My bicycle crash, the shingles episode and my mom's accident were all preceded by either an encounter with Virda or a mention of Aral's Shoe Repair. There seemed to be a pattern but, based on my history of magical thinking, it was probably correlation and not causation.

No amount of rationalization could change the fact of my anger about receiving the lilies. I had a strong urge to break something. When I was young and couldn't contain my anger, I would take an empty bottle or a jar down to the basement and shatter it in the corner. The breaking glass had a calming effect as did the cleanup after.

"They want to observe you for a little while longer," I reminded her.

"What's the difference if I sleep at home or here? About five thousand dollars, that's what."

It was no use trying to convince her to stay in the hospital. Even though she was still slurring her words, I knew better than to argue with her. Kevin and I helped her in and out of the car, then into her bed.

Kevin had to get to work, so I looked after her for the day. She was awake just long enough to sip some water and eat half a sandwich, then she sank back to sleep. During one of her in-between moments, she said something about Shonda.

"That girl...just my sweetest friend."

I baked a coffee cake from a box and I brought it to Shonda's door. She laughed when I did a bad impression of my mom's sentiment.

When I returned, I heard the rhythmic breathing of my mom sleeping in the next room so I took a moment to flop on the sofa and try to remember my own name. It occurred to me that I should get some sleep but my mind continued to whirl in concentric loops. Most of the flowers on the coffee table were still crisp and colorful but the three lilies from Virda were already brown and droopy.

I grabbed a broom, a dustpan and a bottle of my favorite soda. I chugged the soda as I walked down the alley and, when I was far enough away that I was sure my mom wouldn't hear, I delivered the empty vessel to the sidewalk.

# 8

## WIZARD SPELLS

There was five hundred and twenty dollars in my savings account and about sixty in checking. I went to an ATM on the way to pick up Miguel. I hesitated at the ATM. Part of me didn't want to include Miguel in this madness. That was my first instinct. My second instinct was that I needed his help with the tech part of my plan, which I had sketched on a page of a spiral bound notebook.

After explaining my plan, he got the overall intent. I handed him the stack of cash.

"Is it enough?" I asked.

"I think so. What are you going to do with the nanny cam?"

"I want to spy on a shoemaker. You can keep whatever's left."

He gave me a worried look but we sealed the deal with a hand slap fist bump.

We filled a basket at a quirky surplus store frequented by high science teachers, bored teens and wacky dads, then proceeded to a specialty tech store down the street for the expensive stuff.

After buying the gear, we returned to my mom's house, made coffee and got to work. We started by cutting some of the threads between the two front panels of my blue baseball hat with a razor blade. The hat was a perfect match for the one on Aral's coat rack. I created

a small hole for the camera then Miguel installed the wireless camera in such a way that the tiny lens was almost invisible. He also added a pill-sized microphone inside the bill and a coin-sized battery in place of the fabric-covered button on top. While he finished sewing, I created a new cloud storage account and downloaded the pro version of an app that Miguel said would be good for streaming the audio and video. It connected wirelessly to my phone but had a limited range, so we also bought a signal amplifier that I could keep in my car. I ran some tests to make sure the image was clear but kept it brief to preserve the battery life.

It was 11:30 p.m. when Miguel guided my car into the alley that led to the shop. He turned off the headlights, shifted the transmission into neutral for maximum stealth and we coasted up beside Aral's dumpster. The shop was dark inside.

I left the car door open and walked around to the west side of the building. I waited for a lull in traffic, took the yellowish Cream City brick from my backpack and smashed it through the window. Shards of glass rained down on the sidewalk and window ledge. I climbed up and darted my arm into the shop, swapping the baseball hat on the coat rack with the identical hat from my head. Twenty seconds later I was back in the car and we were gone.

The pulse of adrenaline made us giddy. We circled back after we calmed down, parking a safe distance away. The shop was still dark but the exterior was visible in the streetlight.

"I don't need to get arrested," Miguel said.

The streetlight flickered as a semi truck whooshed past. There was a sound like broken ice falling into a metal bowl and the street lights came back to reveal an unbroken window. We got a good look at it but struggled to understand. The window had been reassembled into an unbroken panel that reflected passing headlights and taillights on Howell Avenue. We were dumbfounded.

"What the hell, David!"

His hand gripped the keys that were still in the ignition. His eyes were wild with fear.

After a few minutes of disbelief, the police hadn't arrived and no one seemed aware of either our act of vandalism nor the impossible reality of a reconstituted window. Miguel started the car and drove away in full meltdown mode.

"It's too crazy for me. What kind of shoes do they make in there?"

One of us needed to stay calm and it had to be me. I tamped down my own disbelief about the window and my guilt for involving my friend in such a scene.

"Hey. Pull over and let me drive."

I drove us to a 24-hour restaurant to collect ourselves. We ordered breakfast and said nothing to each other for several minutes. He alternated between staring out the window and pushing at his hash browns with a fork. I offered him the hot sauce and then checked my phone. My mom had texted me something about a show on PBS, reassuring me that she was feeling better.

"I draw the line at black magic," Miguel said.

"Everything is going to be alright."

"How did they do it? Was it like...wizard spells?"

"I don't know but you don't need to worry about it."

He repeated himself. Wizard spells. Black magic. Special effects.

"Let's just take some deep breaths. I want to tell you how much I appreciate your help. I wouldn't ask for it if I didn't need it and I couldn't have done this without you. If you ever need anything, I owe you. The last thing I want to say is that we have to trust each other to keep this a secret. Cone of silence."

"Don't ask me to do anything like that again. I'm out."

I dropped him off and went back to my mom's house. When I got there, Kevin and Daniela were on different ends of the sofa. Kevin was embedded in a pile of pillows, snoring like a chainsaw. Daniela was awake and upright, leaned over one of the three prayer candles I purchased months before. It was the white candle with skull on the label.

The flame danced light on Daniela's face as she hummed a song. She looked up at me and continued singing for a time, then eventually stopped. A distant car alarm pulsed in the night.

"I'm glad you and Miguel are okay. I had a dream that someone pushed you guys into a pit."

# 9

## DANIELA KNOWS THINGS

When my brother told me he was going to marry a woman whom he had known only a few months, I told him it was a bad idea. He had been through a divorce only a year prior to his engagement and I worried that it was a rebound thing and a big mistake. I convinced myself that he was heading for a pitfall.

I was wrong. Daniela turned out to be a remarkably empathetic person who genuinely loved my brother. Their connection became a template for all future relationships in my own life.

I later learned that Daniela had overcome an extra measure of hardship in her life that included losing both of her parents at a very young age and a battle with cancer. She was raised in Chicago by her brother Ossy who practiced law down there.

She cupped her hands around the candle flame.

"What was that song?" I asked while pulling the lever to engage the recliner's footrest.

"When I was younger, my brother hummed Yoruba prayer songs to put me to sleep."

"I like it."

"Thanks. I have no idea what it means."

"What is Yoruba?"

"It's a kind of religion my mother and father practiced. I don't really know that much about it to be honest. Ossy could tell you more."

"He's really funny. I talked to him at your wedding."

I considered how Ossy took care of his little sister and how my relationship with Kevin was nothing like that. We fought all the time as kids and then continued that dynamic as teens. We didn't actually become friends until we were adults.

A memory popped into my head. It was Christmas break. I ruined one of Kevin's sweaters and he retaliated by soaking my room with a high-powered water rifle. I invited him to step outside so we could have a proper fistfight. As soon as he stepped out, I locked him out in the cold. He ran around to the back door just as I locked the dead bolt, then to the garage door which I also locked. He screamed at me through the windows while I smiled and gave him the finger.

My mind snapped back to the night's events and Miguel's freakout.

"Are you okay?" she asked.

"Yeah. Just tired."

"I had this crazy nightmare and told your brother that we needed to come over here and make sure you were alright. Is Miguel okay?"

"Yeah, I just dropped him off. He's fine."

Daniela reached for the other two prayer candles and set them next to the red one so she could read the labels.

"Why do you have these?"

"I don't know, I just liked the art."

"Are you sure?"

# 10

## PROTECTION FROM ENEMIES

The room was empty when I woke up in the recliner. I shuffled towards the kitchen for coffee.

Daniela was garnishing Bloody Marys while Kevin flipped sausages with tongs. Mom sat at the table talking about the wasps. She called them "little fart faces" which I found amusing. Kevin said he had drowned them with the hose.

We dispersed after breakfast. I called my manager Bon from the car to apologize for my sudden exit the previous Monday. He was very understanding. He told me about the time his mother had a blood clot and how he had done the same thing. Also, I could pick up my paycheck. I sent a text to Miguel to let him know my mom was okay. I offered to send him some videos and he responded with, "Please don't."

I grabbed my backpack and headed out. Phase two of the plan was pretty easy. The shop was closed when I stopped my car on an adjacent street. I plugged in the signal amplifier, loaded the app, and was soon recording the sights and sounds inside the shop through the hidden hat camera. There were long periods of nothing followed by several scenes that were real mind-melters. I couldn't parse the reality of the recordings.

I captured nine clips, about twenty minutes of footage in total,

before driving to pick up my check. Bon was watching soccer on his laptop when I entered his office. My thoughts were still wild with disbelief but I managed to keep it together.

My mom was vacuuming when I got home. We ate tacos from paper plates when she was finished and she told me that my dad had called. He heard about the wasp incident on social media.

"He's a doofus but at least he called."

To use the words "fart faces" and "doofus" in one day made me realize how adorable and hilarious my mom really was. She had a way of cutting right through my anxiety.

I relit the *Protection from Enemies* candle and went downstairs to the basement where I watched the surveillance videos again and again. They defied belief.

The first clip featured the child I had glimpsed through the door and tried to photograph. It revealed that she was not a child but a small woman with braided brown hair and a prominent nose. The footage showed her passing by the camera singing a Whitney Houston song.

In the next clip, Aral tossing two handfuls of peeled carrots to three naked, green monsters with big toothy mouths. Yes, naked green monsters. Their crunching was comically loud. I had never seen root vegetables eaten so fast or with so much gusto.

In the last video, Virda yelled and jabbed her finger into her brother's chest as he stood stoic.

Were the cobblers just messing with me? Was it some kind of hoax that I was meant to see and tell others about? I tried to convince myself that it was real but I needed a second opinion. I exported the clip of the monsters eating carrots and thought about sending it to Miguel. With one impulsive tap, it was sent.

The sun had almost set when my phone pinged, signifying a response from Miguel.

His text read, "Don't send any more of these. I don't want ANY MORE CRAZY TIMES!! (mind blown emoji)"

"I'm coming over," I texted back, "Put some pants on."

I was en route to Miguel's house when someone inside the car spoke my name. It shocked me to the extent that I swerved and nearly hit a man on a bicycle. My heart was punching like a clenched fist. When

Aral's face appeared in my rearview mirror, my instincts turned from fear to aggression.

"Get out!"

Aral reached for something in his chest pocket. A weapon? I didn't need to find out. I jerked the wheel hard to the right at the next intersection and saw him move past the rearview mirror. Had he been buckled into the seat, he might not have been thrown with such force. Seat belts were apparently something he didn't use.

He shouted some words that sounded like, *"Pie duke button fool"* but I wasn't listening. I was full of adrenaline and rage. I started to dial 9-1-1 with one hand and Aral snatched my phone with remarkable speed.

"Hey!"

"David please—"

I accelerated then turned a sharp left on Clement Avenue. *Kalump.* My passenger piled hard against the door. His hand reached forward and yanked the wheel, directing the car into an alley. I resisted, stomped the brakes and felt his weight against the back of my seat. The car stopped, pinning a wheeled trash tote against a garage door. My phone landed on the passenger's side floor mat.

"Do not fear," Aral said and regained his proper orientation in the rear view mirror.

Before he could say another word, the heel of my hand slammed the center of the steering wheel, releasing a long horn blast.

The rear door opened and Aral was gone. I let off the horn.

A father and his young daughter, presumably out for a walk, held hands and stared at the car with open mouths.

I got out and asked if they saw someone run away.

"A goat just jumped out of your car," the girl said.

# 11

ROAD OPENER

I needed to think about my next move. I texted Miguel in the early afternoon to say I wouldn't be coming over after all and I'd explain later. What just happened? Was it a murder attempt? I told myself that nobody hides in someone's car just to have a friendly conversation. I debated whether calling the police was a smart course of action considering the fact that I had also broken the law.

Rhythmic thumping indicated steps and music upstairs. Mom must have been exercising or dancing.

I examined Aral's blue hat that I had swapped from his coat tree and found a few long white hairs. A search revealed that there was a company in Sacramento that would conduct DNA analysis on hair samples for about ninety dollars. The hairs were soon in a plastic bag which I slipped into in a big yellow envelope along with a signed consent form and a check for the required amount. Six stamps later, it was in the mailbox with the flag up.

When I returned from the mailbox, I noticed the *Protection From Enemies* candle was gone from the coffee table. I asked my mom about it and she said she had thrown it away.

"Why would you do that? It was for our protection!"

I looked in the trash and saw the spent candle covered by wads of paper and something sticky.

"Don't take it out of the trash. That's gross."

How wretched I had become: a grown man living with his mother and rooting through her trash. Pathetic.

I went down to the basement, lit the green *Road Opener* candle and set it on a coaster. It smelled like pine needles. Then I stuffed Aral's blue hat in one of the kitchenette drawers and texted Miguel with my usual greeting: the alien emoji.

No response. He must have been mad at me and I didn't blame him. I told myself that the next time I saw him I would apologize and double-promise to leave him out of any crazy times.

My mom called down to me, "David! Your friend is here!"

Light brown boots, not red sneakers, descended the carpeted staircase.

Seeing it was Aral and not Miguel, I prepared myself for a melee. I lifted a barstool as he approached and aimed it at him as if he was a feral beast.

"Please calm yourself," he suggested.

"What do you want?" I shout-whispered, not yet ready to worry my mother, "You have five seconds before I hit you with something heavy."

He was wearing the blue baseball hat with the camera installed in it. A long tube was slung over his shoulder. He didn't look like an assailant but I couldn't be sure.

"I am here as a friend."

"What's that?" I pointed at the tube.

"Tea," he said.

"Why were you in my car?"

"I want a conversation — to help you. Let us have tea."

"I don't need your help. There's no good reason to sneak into someone's car and pop out like that."

"It was a mistake," he said as he pulled the barstool from my hands and sat on it, "My reason was to meet you in a place where she could not see."

In a few twisting motions he produced two tea cups and a pitcher from the cylinder.

"My sister watches you but she cannot see into a car," he said.

"Please drink tea with me. The tea will hide us from her view."

He sipped from his cup as if to prove it wasn't poisoned. The tea was as good as I remembered. Jasmine. I thought about the girl who said a goat jumped out of my car and a nervous tremor shook some tea from my cup.

"How did you fix the window?"

"A simple mending. I am not here to talk about that. I want to break the *fledrif*."

"*fledrif*?" I sneered.

"The spell. It tells Virda when you speak of us delivers misfortune."

"So tell her to leave us alone."

"I did tell her. But you and Miguel continue to speak of us and now she has taken him."

"Wait, what?"

"Virda has taken Miguel. That is why I come to you."

"I'm calling the cops."

He snatched my phone like he did in my car. The speed of his hand was incredible. When I moved to take it back, he slipped sideways and shoved my chest with an economy of movement that demonstrated a level of strength and dexterity I couldn't match. He slid my phone into his pocket.

"I know she is wrong, so I come to help you. My sister is not evil. She has been hurt and holds tight to bitterness. Wears it like armor. It makes her do bad things."

My mind couldn't think fast enough. She kidnapped Miguel. My thoughts were an angry mob pushing against a door. I grabbed the nearest object — Papa Chuck's phone lamp — from a storage shelf and hurled it at him. Aral deflected the lamp and it shattered on the cinder block wall. The hardware and lampshade fell to the floor in a shower of ceramic shards.

"Is everything okay down there?" my mom asked from the top of the steps.

Although I considered shouting a warning or asking for emergency assistance, I didn't do so. The implications of that choice seemed grim.

"We're okay! I dropped my cup. I'll clean it up."

Aral raised a finger, as if to ask me "please wait just one second."

He then proceeded to do something that held my attention so fully that the momentum of my anger turned into amazement. He gestured at the pieces of broken lamp with both hands, levitating the debris in a cloud of jagged bits. His manipulations puzzled the lamp pieces in midair, filling the spaces between the power cord and the bulb assembly and fusing into the lamp's original shape. The seams were smoothed by the time it fell into his hands. I couldn't help but laugh a little when he placed it back in its original location on the shelf.

The spectacle had held my attention but I needed to find out where Virda had taken Miguel.

"Where is he?"

"I will take you to him but first we must break Virda's spell."

He reached inside his front overall pocket and produced a three-inch paper airplane like the one Virda had placed in Papa Chuck's shoe, then handed it to me.

"Unfold it, fold it again and burn it in the candle."

There were curly, multicolored characters written on the unfolded paper. The day's madness taxed my ability to focus. Although I always believed that fantastic creatures lived among us, now that I was facing one in my mom's basement, I felt both confused and ridiculous.

"Please do as I ask," Aral urged.

I folded the paper back into an airplane and held it over the candle flame. It combusted in a single flash that singed my fingers and startled me into letting go. The smoldering remains drifted to the floor trailed by a thin tendril of smoke.

# 12

## FINDING FLURGLE

Aral shifted nervously in his seat as I drove us back to the cobbler shop. On the way there, I demanded that he relinquish my phone and he refused. I lost my temper, swearing and saying some nasty things that he didn't understand, which caused him to snicker at me. His laughter made me more angry and thus made him laugh harder. It felt like I might erupt into flames.

"If I don't tell my boss that I'm not coming in today, he'll know something's up. I'm always on time and never miss a shift."

They were lies, plus I didn't have to work until the next day.

Aral warned, "If you call the police, Virda will do very bad things."

"I won't call the police! Just give it back."

He put the phone in my hand and gave me a meaningful stare. I checked my messages. Still nothing from Miguel. I texted him again as Aral tried to read the screen.

"Let me know if you get this? I want to know if ur ok."

We parked next to the recycle dumpster. It was normal business hours but the place was dark and locked up. We went inside and snapped the lock shut behind us.

"Hello?" he called out, "*Unri?*"

Hearing no response, he signaled for me to follow.

"Let us drink water before we go."

He also urged me to use the bathroom before our trip, just like Papa Chuck would have done.

We passed through the doorway to the next room where the toothy vegetable-eaters and the tiny child with the buckle shoes had been caught on video. On one wall was a bookshelf packed tight with hardcover volumes and on the opposite wall was another shelf stocked with stoppered bottles filled with colorful liquids, powders, feathers and other assorted components. A vintage TV/VCR combo unit was mounted up in the corner and held a half-ejected VHS tape of *Television's Funniest Bloopers*. There was also a worn leather armchair with a big wooden chest in front of it. Aral raised the lid of the chest and pulled from it a glass orb hanging in a crocheted net.

We then proceeded through another door and down a stairway into the basement. When we reached a dark room on the south side of the building, Aral tapped the glass orb twice with his forefinger and it glowed like a lightbulb. It illuminated the wall where large older masonry was interrupted by a section of smaller bricks. I had seen a similar pattern in the basement wall at Fancy Dan's when I dumped the mop water. A wave of Aral's hand caused the smaller bricks to fall at our feet, exposing a tunnel as tall as a refrigerator and wide as a coffin.

It wasn't far-fetched to think his plan was to lock me in a dungeon or feed me to the toothy green monsters but if murder was his goal, why would he care about my hydration or ask me if I needed to use the bathroom? For that matter, if I thought he was leading me to my death, why was I following him at all? I guess it felt like my only choice.

We ducked our heads to shuffle our way across the dirt floors of the tunnel, past the improvised wooden trusses that supported the ceiling and through a series of intersecting shafts. Along the route were a few bricked-over sections of wall in the shape of doorways. I recalled rumors about bootlegger tunnels below Lion Horse and other Milwaukee establishments that were used to transport booze during prohibition. I couldn't help but be enthralled at what I was seeing.

There was a blank wall at the end of the passageway. Aral pushed the right edge and the wall hinged outward, dropping dirt into a deep chasm full of stench and echoey drips.

"Now we climb."

I followed him down, descending the dewy rungs of a steel utility ladder. After a minute, I looked up and saw a manhole cover with spears of light streaming through small holes. It was about the size of a quarter, which provided a vague idea of our current depth.

Farther down I saw a pipe issuing steam. My fingers were pruned from the dampness and I almost lost grip on the rungs at that point. Afraid that I might not survive a fall, I used my forearms to lock myself to the ladder and tried to dry my hands on my shirt. The manhole above had become a distant dot when my work uglies met solid ground again.

"It smells terrible down here."

"You smell the deeper tunnels," he said, holding his hands toward a moist concrete wall as though he were preparing to catch someone in a trust fall. The inset border of a rectangle became apparent and the slab swung open on a hidden pivot. It revealed a different sort of tunnel, this one lined with gray-brown cobblestones of varying size. The floor reminded me vaguely of the *Streets of Old Milwaukee* exhibit at the Milwaukee Public Museum I was obsessed with as a kid. The door closed behind us, sealing out the foul odors and replacing them with the scent of a closet long ignored. We hurried down a hallway and then another, stopping at a stone staircase that spiraled downward. The sound of distant footsteps reverberated below.

The idea of another person in the tunnels gave me a dose of terror but that wasn't the only reason I hesitated. It also occurred to me that dying underground would mean my friends and family might never know what happened to me. I snagged the back of Aral's overalls to prevent him from proceeding down the stairs.

"Wait...where exactly is Miguel?"

"Muskego."

The answer went past my threshold for nonsense.

"That can't be right."

"First Muskego, then *Hone Cheval*."

I was no expert in subterranean transit but it sounded ludicrous. I could have driven us to Muskego in about twenty minutes. Maybe the word meant something different in his native tongue. I was suspicious his answer was meant to distract me from his actual plan: to lead me to a place where no one could hear me scream.

He started down the helix of stairs and it felt like a good time to start recording with the hat camera. After he had traveled a full loop downward, I started the camera and returned my phone to my pocket. It was 4:40 p.m. and my power level was at 40%.

Aral waited for me to catch up and after resuming our descent, I could hear the clapping footsteps echoing closer. Aral was unfazed and continued down the stairs. The sound turned out to be the footfalls of a green pedestrian of the same species as the carrot-munching figures in my surveillance video. The figure clapped up the stairs with familiar roped sandals tied to oversized feet but stopped still when they saw us.

The stranger was adorable like a plush toy brought to life. We shared several seconds of mutual fascination, examining each others' features and peering their big yellow eyes into my beady browns. Their long orange hair was tied in a ponytail behind large ears and they wore overalls with small tools in the chest pocket.

"*Dernod da, Flurgle,*" Aral said in an upbeat tone.

"*Dernod da,*" the stranger replied without taking their eyes off me.

We continued down the stairs. As I passed the stranger, my forearm brushed against the velvety fuzz on their little arm. The tactile sensation changed the quasi-dream into a palpable experience and I shuddered, scratching my arm to remove the tickly feeling.

"Flurgle is a special hob," Aral said, "Takes a rest upstairs and watches TV tapes."

"A hob."

"Hobs are goblins with gnomish blood. Or gnomes with goblish blood. They are clever and kind."

"Seems nice," I mustered.

We reached the bottom of the stairs and stood before a broad wooden door with a rounded top. I could swear that I heard the electro-mechanical pings and clacks of a pinball machine from somewhere on the other side.

"Stay behind me until we reach the *kydwil fil drysa,*" Aral said, "Huh?"

"The Hollow of a Thousand Doors."

# 13

## PHANTOM LIMBS

Aral handed me the glowing bulb in order to free both hands and sort through a series of large keys on a three-inch ring. Again I heard familiar clacks and pings behind the door, this time they were accompanied by synthesized voices.

"Is that a pinball machine?"

After he had placed a key in the door, Aral fished for something in his pockets. He produced a stoppered bottle the size of a lipstick and shook some pink powder into his hand, then threw it in my face. The bitter salt burned my eyes and nose. I coughed like crazy.

"We must be sure they don't smell your stench."

The stuff had gone into my sinuses and I couldn't cough it out.

"This will mask your stink...and disguise your form."

"This is (sniff) too much. I can't do it."

Aral looped a rope around my waist and knotted it. It was exceptionally tight.

"Gah! What's that for?"

"Now you must be quiet. I cannot hide your sounds. Better if my people do not hear or see you."

He pulled the door open, releasing a rush of warm air and a fragrance like pungent vinegar. The smell stunned me into compliance

and a tug from my waist tether got me moving.

My first steps inside the massive chamber were uncoordinated. I now saw that my chest had somehow been made to resemble a plump canvas bag, not unlike the laundry bags used by military personnel, and my lower body had morphed into a wooden wagon. Only when I ran my fingertips over the skin of my face did I realize that it was an illusion rather than an actual physical transformation. I could feel my phantom limbs and verify the sensation of feet on the floor but the lack of visual feedback made walking an uncoordinated enterprise.

Just inside the door, against a wall on our right, was a flashing pinball machine being played by a goatman; that is, a fur-covered humanoid with a goat's head and legs. Then I recognized the backglass.

"Pirate's Booty!"

Aral jerked the rope to shut me up but it didn't lessen my excitement about seeing the same pinball machine taken from the Lion Horse. Was it the very one?

The high ceilings of the space were supported by giant pillars, each equipped at the top with canoe-sized bulbs that bathed the room in yellow light. Winged insects zipped around the lights while a mix of characters circulated at ground level. There was a long table that appeared to be an assembly line, with a variety of workers using implements to complete steps in the construction of gizmos that looked like golf balls made of pale gray metal. Some of the workers looked human and whereas others were similar to the goatman playing pinball. Other, shorter beings looked similar to the buckle shoes gal in my video or like bearded garden gnomes come to life. There were also several hobs like Flurgle scattered throughout the room.

One figure, a smiling behemoth with glasses, towered over the others and carried an overstuffed canvas bag identical to the one I myself resembled. The bag was connected by a hose to a device in the giant's hand. When a hob at an assembly table summoned the behemoth, they plodded over and connected the handheld device to the summoner's metal gadgets one at a time, and pulled a trigger to fill each one in turn with whatever mystical goop was in the bag.

I was distracted from that process by something that sped across my field of vision. It was a hob towing what appeared to be a small rickshaw. Noticing other hobs racing around the room with similar rigs, I could see the trailers were not rickshaws but wagons with long handles attached to wide leather belts worn by the drivers. They were couriers. Some delivered parts and assembled devices while others transported refreshments: tea kettles, bottles, cups and snacks.

"*Dernod da, Figda!*" Aral said to a passing hob who smiled in response before rolling a wagon wheel over the pencil-like bones at the front of my left foot.

"Agh!" I blurted, causing Aral to give my waist tether another yank.

"*Pardoon,*" the hob said, thinking they bumped Aral's wagon.

I tried to stay quiet as we passed through an open door and down a curved hallway, but it hurt like crazy. The extent of my limp and the daggers of pain made me dread the gore I would find inside my shoe.

We arrived at another wooden door like the one we last entered. On the door was a jagged symbol I didn't recognize. Through that door was another immense cavern, this one much darker and composed of chalky, calcium-like stone. Above were stalactites studded with pink and blue gems that radiated dim, pastel-colored light. There were narrow walkways that snaked into the distance and connected to other walkways that branched off, terminating in similar doors bearing their own unique symbols.

The illusion of the laundry sack dissipated like smoke and I was relieved to see my normal, broken self.

The light of Aral's glowing bulb-in-a-net illuminated our steps as we set off down the track. My injury made it difficult to walk with confidence on a catwalk that was no wider than my shoulders and lacked railings of any kind. We crept onward for what seemed like an hour or more.

The walkway became even more narrow. If there were a location on the journey where I was most likely to die, this was it. No sooner had the thought of imminent death entered my mind when I stumbled beyond the margin. A jolt of terror was punctuated by an abrupt stop as Aral gripped with both hands the rope tied around my waist. His reflexes had prevented me from plummeting into darkness but doing so had forced him to drop the glowing orb that had lit our way. It fell into the abyss, shrinking into a white dot before it disappeared with a muffled blip.

# 14

## THE WILDS OF MUSKEGO

The balance of our time in the Hollow of a Thousand Doors was a dim affair that doubled my fear of slipping into the ravine. I chose to shuffle with extreme care as we advanced down the main walkway and negotiated an offshoot path that culminated in yet another door. Up close I could see that the door was labeled with three carrots.

After a rattle of keys and a click, a blast of daylight shone through the opening. We crossed over into a stand of trees where I stood for a moment, breathing in the ambient smell of the forest. Aral closed the door, which had a curved, craggy exterior that blended into the trunk of the rotund maple into which it was embedded. I had to laugh at the confounding physics of a vast cavern within a tree but there was no time to marvel. Aral was already trotting down a trail and I needed to check my phone. The power level was down to 10% and the time was 4:49 p.m. How could what felt like an hour spent underground take only six minutes? It made no damn sense at all. A look at the map showed we were indeed in Muskego. Even more than the other bewildering aspects of the journey, I still remain baffled by the disparities between the geography and chronology of that period.

A small lake glistened through the trees. Thumb-typing in midstride, I texted Kevin. The last time I got into trouble, he came to the

Kettle Moraine and convinced the park ranger that my Sasquatch trap wasn't a poaching attempt. He said that was the last time but it was worth a shot. I also included some instructions in case the worst-case scenario were to materialize. Right before Aral shouted for me to hurry up, I sent a screenshot of a map showing our location and the login for my cloud account.

"My foot is killing me. How much farther?"

"Not far."

That's what Papa Chuck used to say when, in fact, a significant distance remained. Any pressure on my left foot was excruciating so I leaned against a tree to take the weight off for a minute.

Aral protested.

"Understand that we must hurry, David."

"One more question?"

"No questions. I take you to find Miguel. Let us go now."

"Why come here and open a shop where you could be discovered?"

He was exasperated and exhaled hard before answering.

"We need materials. Things like aluminum and magnesium — like from recycled cans — are plenty here and very rare at home. We use them to make *hoowak* and we grow food in Hone Cheval."

"Wait. Hoowak? What's a hoowak?"

He said nothing and handed me a fallen branch with a two-pronged fork on one end. I hobbled after him using it as a crutch.

After another few minutes of hiking, the cobbler stopped and flailed his arms like he had walked into a spider's web. It took me a moment to realize that he was miming his hands over the surface of an invisible wall. My sense of what was and was not ridiculous had become so distorted that I didn't even laugh about being in the wilderness, leaning on a wizard staff, watching an alien cobbler act like a mime.

My phone vibrated, indicating either an incoming message or battery death just as Aral dug his fingers into open air. He peeled back what I thought was the real landscape like a tent flap and revealed yet another hidden world behind an illusory curtain.

Years before, I read an article from *Milwaukee Record* about a mythical Wisconsin village called Haunchyville. It was allegedly home to a group of reclusive circus performers who were protected by a murderous albino man. The albino defended his enclave from intruders with either an axe or a shotgun. Or maybe he was more of a pitchfork guy. Anyway, it seemed probable that Haunchyville and Hone Cheval were the same place.

After ushering me past the curtain, Aral relinquished my crutch and threw more bitter dust in my face. I wheezed as the sack-on-a-cart illusion again took effect.

Inside we found plenty of spectacle but no murderous albino man in sight. The village seemed both idyllic and otherworldly, composed of a few dozen structures of varying size. All were built with stacked blocks and spackled with mud. The roofs were composed of a smooth organic material I couldn't identify. A narrow but smooth path of the same material meandered through the village and encircled a central garden area where villagers tended their crops.

On the opposite side of the garden was circular pool of clear water and beyond was a grove of fruit trees where hobs hung from ropes connected to spools on their belts. They plucked purple fruits and tossed them to two others at ground level who piled them in belt wagons. They all spoke so fast that they sounded like auctioneers. A gnome-like fellow with a mustache and red hat sat on a log in front of a tiny house as three hob children ran past him, kicking a ball. I could have sworn it was Cherry. I wanted to say hello but remembered I had been ordered not to speak. Besides, I was disguised as a big gray sack.

A black and white dog resembling a Welsh corgi was leashed close to one of the stone structures ahead and sniffed the air as we approached. When we approached the dwelling, the dog inspected my bad foot, probably smelling blood. The house had circular windows and two red door panels. Aral untied the dog and lifted it into his arms before going inside.

We stepped into a rustic kitchen, where Virda was leaning over a dining table, inspecting Miguel's smartphone.

A jolt of courage sent me into the room with a determination to find Miguel, but something punched me in the chest, punctuating my search. The thing jutted from my shirt, thin like a pencil but longer. What followed were dark, distorted thoughts about blood on the floor.

# 15

## SORCERY STINKS

The way my mom tells it, Kevin and Daniela brought her some homemade chicken stew. Upon entering the house, Daniela began asking about bad smells.

"She kept asking me 'do you smell that?' I thought she was talking about that green candle you left burning in the basement. By the way David, you could have burned the house down. But she said the stink wasn't from the candle. She brought up that old lamp from downstairs and had us smell it. I was freaked out. I thought she was having a psychotic episode."

When I asked Daniela what happened, she gave a similar account.

"Kevin and your mother thought I was cuckoo but it was just so stinky. I couldn't believe they didn't smell it. It was like old seafood, but worse. Then Kevin got your text."

My mom said she was very close to calling the local police department to request assistance. I'm not sure how things would have played out had she done so. No doubt the officers could find missing persons but I wasn't sure if they would take the call seriously or whether anyone without Daniela's almost supernatural sense of smell could have sniffed out Hone Cheval. It's also likely that, without a timely distraction, I would have been killed.

# 16

## JAGGED WORDS

Returning to consciousness was confusing. There was an itchy feeling on my chest that demanded a scratch. When I scratched it, I felt a damp hole in my T-shirt. There was an odd rattle in my lungs that made me want to cough. My brain was fogged like a hangover but my foot felt better than ever.

"I put arrows in you but you are alive," someone said, "Aral fixed you."

My senses were still recalibrating. On my left was a familiar little woman with brown hair and tiny black buckle shoes. She sat holding the seat of her chair and kicked her legs idly beneath her poncho. Beside her was an ornate bow and a quiver full of feathery arrows, apparently the real thing even though their size made them look like toys.

"Virda told me to kill you if you attack."

"I didn't attack" I said between groans.

"You did."

I lifted myself into the chair next to hers. The floor came into focus and I saw it was tiled with flat stones and bottle caps, damp from a recent cleaning.

"I'm David."

"I know. I am Wick."

I could hear Aral and Virda's voices in another part of the house, arguing.

"What they are saying in there?"

"Virda is angry. She says David will die."

Wick's cheery demeanor didn't match her words at all. For someone who had put two arrows in my chest, I found my would-be killer to be very friendly. I wondered if she might help me find Miguel.

"Where is my friend?"

She pointed at Miguel's clothes which were folded neatly and set on a side table. The black and white corgi lay under the table near Miguel's red sneakers and wagged his tail when I looked over.

"Those are his clothes. Where is my friend?"

She continued to point.

A week ago I wouldn't have been able to cope with or grasp such a thing but after all that I had seen that day, I was prepared for the realization that Virda had turned Miguel into an adorable corgi.

Our phones were on the table surrounded by pieces of black glass. The cobblers had smashed the screens with some blunt object so they could peer inside.

"They were looking for your scroll. Did not find it," Wick said.

I pushed a triangular bit of glass with my finger.

"I'm glad all of my stuff is on the cloud."

"The cloud?"

"Yeah—all of my photos and videos. I keep them on the cloud so I don't lose them."

"They stay in a cloud?" she tweedled her fingers in the air to pantomime a cloud floating in the sky.

"That's right. I made videos with a camera in Aral's hat. They're like Flurgle's TV tapes. I even have a video of you singing a Whitney Houston song."

She seemed flattered but then paused for a beat.

"Aral's hat makes TV tapes?"

"Yes. He's wearing it right now."

She wrinkled her forehead and considered the implications, then collected her archery gear.

"Stay," she said before running down the hallway.

I sat back in my chair, listened, and pet Miguel's fur, which felt strange yet comforting.

Aral and Virda's argument paused long enough for Wick to deliver the report. Virda's voice shouted with renewed fervor.

Wick and Virda were looking down at me a moment later. Virda had the blue baseball cap in her hand, shaking it in my face and asking what I had done.

"We put a camera and a microphone in Aral's hat."

She threw the hat on the floor, "You camera us and send it to a cloud? What are these lies?"

"It's the truth."

She balled her fists as her tantrum grew. Wick looked to Virda with concern and then over at me. Two invisible hands seized my spine like a broom handle and bent me sideways. The pain was intense.

Aral emerged from the hallway with a red welt on his cheek.

"Will you kill them all?" he asked his sister.

The pressure on my back abated.

"Fool!" Virda hollered in my face, spitting a little, then swept the smartphone debris from the table.

"I was curious," I explained, "The cobbling was done so well. I wanted to understand it."

Virda let out a stream of jagged words I couldn't understand and stormed down the hallway cursing the universe and beyond.

Aral scooped up the baseball cap and plopped himself down on the chair beside me. He studied the hat, poking his finger into the tiny camera lens before he looked up and presented it to me for confirmation.

"Pretty clever, eh?"

"Pretty clever."

He continued to examine the hat.

"I will delete the videos if you let us go," I offered.

"This word 'delete.' What does it mean?"

"They will go away forever."

He reached into a pocket and produced an envelope folded in half. He presented it for me to see. The address of the DNA analysis company in Sacramento was written in my handwriting.

"We cannot trust you," he waved the envelope, "You would reveal us to science and ruin everything we have worked for."

"You took that out of my mailbox? That's a federal offense."

He pointed a finger, "You broke my window with a brickstone!"

"You ambushed me in my car!"

"I try to help you!"

"Like you helped Miguel?"

"I healed your chest!"

"He's a dog!"

Aral stood and opened the door of the wood stove. He tossed both the hat and the envelope into the fire then joined his sister in the back room. The plastic produced a horrible odor so I closed the stove door. There was a sizzle when the batteries burst open.

# 17

## CEASE ALL EVIL

The hushed voices of our captors indicated that another tense negotiation was taking place in another room. Wick and the two siblings reemerged after a few minutes.

"Virda agrees to let you live," Aral said, "but you must remain here… as friends."

"Friends?"

Virda crossed her arms and leaned against the door jamb, "You can choose any small creature you like as long as it fits in a cage. Would you like to be a piglet, a squirrel or a chicken?"

"None of the above."

"You will not like the other options," Virda warned.

"My videos are scheduled to post to my social media accounts tomorrow," I bluffed, "and all my people will see hobs eating carrots, the tunnels, the caverns, the workers making hoowak and lots more. I even have a map showing the location of this village. But I'd rather keep your secret."

Virda grabbed me by the throat with both hands, demonstrating considerable strength. All rhythm left my lungs.

Miguel ran over to us, rapid-fire barking. Aral moved to intervene and she kicked him in the crotch, displaying remarkable dexterity.

"Stop!" Wick shouted at her.

"Suppose I turn your flesh to sugar and let you melt away? Who will you tell then?" Virda snapped at my reddened face as the world began to fade.

Thankfully, she let loose when her attention was drawn by a loud screech followed by a sharp bang. A second, third and fourth screech-bang repeated in the distance.

I fell to the floor, gasping for breath. Virda stepped over me and commanded Aral to "keep them here" before exiting the house to investigate. Wick followed her out the door with her bow and quiver, then Aral stepped out a moment after.

My neck felt as though it had been in the maw of a giant beast but somehow I managed to turn my head and see Aral's wind-up through the open door. He cocked his arm back, revealing the hoowak in his hand, then pitched the spherical metal orb in Virda's direction.

I caught my breath by the time Aral reentered the hovel supporting not Virda, but a bearded gnome-like figure whom he had inadvertently struck with a hoowak.

He helped the unconscious victim into a chair. I could see that the villager wore a secondhand sweatshirt printed with the words "World's Greatest Grandpa." The right shoulder of the sweatshirt was doused with bright blue powder.

"Put Miguel on the table," Aral instructed as he opened a cabinet full of bottles like those I had seen in their Milwaukee shop.

I picked up Miguel the corgi and brought him to the table where Aral was preparing a mixture. He spoke in a serious tone as he mixed blue and red ingredients in a stone bowl.

"I tell you, David. Virda is like many warriors in my family back home. They think they will be safe only when their enemies are dead. For a long time I believed it too. When I made the first hoowak, I told Virda it was a magical grenade to pacify our enemies and calm their anger. She thought it was a good idea until I used one on myself, then she said I was a fool. It gave me the freedom to see that our enemies deserve to live. She chose to remain a warrior but I had changed. Do you understand?"

I nodded.

The purple concoction in Aral's bowl frothed. He poured it on the dog like a ribbon of mustard on a bratwurst. The corgi kicked wildly while Aral kept him from running off the table. The purple fizz spread like lava from a science fair volcano and enveloped Miguel's furry body, splashed around and spilled across the table. There was a pop like a champagne cork and Miguel's original self was on the table in place of the corgi, kicking his legs until he fell off the table. It was pretty gross if I'm being honest, so I looked away and fetched his clothes as he got to his feet.

"*Dernod da,*" a voice said behind us. World's Greatest Grandpa was awake and grinning at the spectacle. Miguel belched in response.

My friend may have looked awful, his hair matted and his shirt sticking to his back, but it was good to see him on two feet.

Hone Cheval was virtually empty when Aral led us outside. Most villagers had sought shelter from the squeals and pops of the bottle rockets that they must have assumed were actual artillery. Others — hobs, goatpeople and gnomes — had ventured out to confront the would-be invaders at the edge of the village.

Aral pushed his way through the mob, parting the crowd and signaling to his comrades with verbal commands and downward gestures. Most lowered their weapons as he requested.

"Who is that?" the cobbler asked me, pointing at Daniela who stood with her hands extended. She seemed to sense the invisible barrier was there without seeing the village beyond. Maybe she could smell it.

"She's a warrior of my people," I said, knowing it sounded corny.

My mom and Kevin were busy lighting the fuses of bottle rockets using the flame of the *Cease All Evil* prayer candle that was stationed on the hood of Kevin's black pickup. Once lit, they loaded the fireworks into two empty beer bottles on the ground and they screeched upward.

Miguel began barking, not having fully recovered from his transformation. It took me a moment to process that he was trying to warn my family of an impending attack. Virda was creeping behind the truck, ready to ambush Kevin.

Aral peeled back the village's invisible barrier and shoved us through. It must have appeared to Daniela that we emerged from empty air, because she rushed over with her eyes wide.

I was way too slow to intercept Virda. She had already flipped Kevin up on the hood, smashing the candle, by the time I snatched one of the empty bottles to use as a weapon. Virda assumed a menacing battle stance while I held the beer bottle in both hands like a pathetic club. She laughed then waved an arm in a spellcasting gesture that hurled Miguel and Daniela toward me like magazines thrown across the room. They slammed into me and the three of us put a significant dent in the passenger side of the truck. We were a tangle of bruised arms and legs.

I scrambled to recover, scared that Virda had attacked my mom in the intervening seconds. Instead I found two figures writhing on the ground. My mother, the taekwondo enthusiast, held Virda, the vengeful shoeshop sorceress, in a rear choke hold with both arms around the assailant's neck and both legs around the assailant's waist. Virda squirmed, trying without success to break free of the grapple. The four of us limped over and stood around the wrestling combatants, unsure about what to do next.

We didn't have to wait long. An object that I can only assume was one of Aral's grenades hit me in the back of the head. Another hit Virda and my mom in the midst of their melee. We were all engulfed by a billowing cloud of potent blue powder. I started laughing, even as the particles stung my eyes and throat. My brain felt like it was dipped in warm maple syrup. The others were laughing too.

The four of us have since tried to corroborate what happened next and there is some agreement amid a lot of disbelief. We all agree that it was Aral who helped us into the truck and got behind the wheel but I'm the only one who remembers Virda hugging her brother before we left.

The ride home from Hone Cheval was like a cab ride after too many cocktails. Daniela's face was pressed to the window and Kevin's head was on my shoulder, snoring in my ear. Miguel laid across our laps. My mom rode shotgun and stared straight ahead in a glazed stupor. It felt safe, not unlike riding in Papa Chuck's station wagon on one of our family road trips to Florida. Also familiar was the turning signal that flashed for an extended period. My mom let out a giggle when our kind chauffeur tried to turn it off and instead engaged the wipers. He asked if we were thirsty — or hungry — and before anyone answered, parked near a late night food truck and returned with tacos for everyone.

# 18

## THE SQUIRREL

I took Miguel to a baseball game a few weeks ago. I had a new job and could afford such things. He let out a bark when our guys hit a double and I tried hard not to laugh because I knew it was evidence of a wound that hadn't healed.

We got a couple of barbecue chicken sandwiches and Miguel revealed that he finally understood why dogs beg for snacks. He said that his sense of smell had returned to normal but he would never forget the sensation of experiencing the world through a dog's nose — like seeing new colors outside of the normal spectrum.

We stayed in the parking lot until it got dark and everyone had cleared out, just talking. That was when Miguel shared a thought that was worth more than eighteen months of biweekly sessions with my the Third Ward therapist. He pointed out a plump gray squirrel raiding the ballpark trash receptacle, and I said "What if it's really a hobgoblin moonlighting as a can collector?" He said that, in an infinite multiverse, everything we can imagine and everything we can't was likely to be true at some point. It wasn't just possible. It was inevitable.